J

PA

Tiger Turcotte
Takes on the
Know-It-All

by
Pansie Hart Flood

pictures by
Amy Wummer

CAROLRHODA BOOKS, INC. / MINNEAPOLIS

This book is available in two editions:
Library binding by Carolrhoda Books, Inc.,
    a division of Lerner Publishing Group
Soft cover by First Avenue Editions,
    an imprint of Lerner Publishing Group
241 First Avenue North
Minneapolis, MN 55401 U.S.A.

Website address: www.carolrhodabooks.com

Library of Congress Cataloging-in-Publication Data

Flood, Pansie Hart.
   Tiger Turcotte Takes on the Know-It-All / by Pansie Hart
Flood ; pictures by Amy Wummer.
      p.   cm.
   Summary: When seven-year-old Tiger Turcotte ends up in
after-school detention with his arch-enemy Donna Overton,
they both learn a lot.
   ISBN: 1–57505–814–6 (lib. bdg. : alk. paper)
   ISBN: 1–57505–900–2 (pbk. : alk. paper)
   [1. Schools—Fiction. 2. Teasing—Fiction. 3. Names,
Personal—Fiction. 4. Friendship—Fiction. 5. Racially mixed
people—Fiction.] I. Wummer, Amy, ill. II. Title.
PZ7.F66185Ti 2005
[Fic]—dc22   2004004729

Manufactured in the United States of America
1 2 3 4 5 6 – JR – 10 09 08 07 06 05

CONTENTS

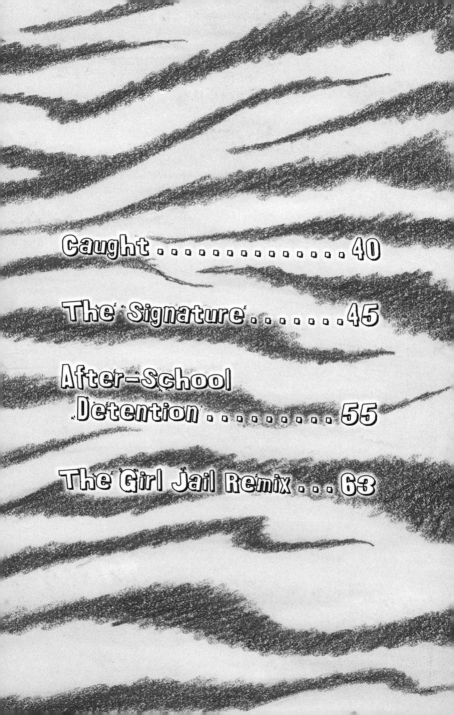

The Accident

Second grade isn't for babies.
There's a lot to get used to, like
practice tests, riding the bus, leaving
school without getting stepped on
by big kids, and silly girls.

My name is Tiger Turcotte.
There's a lot of things I like about
second grade. Donna Overton isn't
one of those things. She's always
bugging me about silly stuff.

During lunch a few days ago, Donna said I was trying to break line in front of her. Another day, she said I was sticking my tongue out at her. It's easy to see that the girl has never liked me. Well, I don't

like her either! She's a know-it-all and always trying to get everyone in trouble.

Today I had a great day until it was time to leave. Too many kids were trying to cram through the door. Somebody pushed me, and I bumped into Donna. Yuck! Girl germs got on my favorite t-shirt.

Donna fell straight to the ground. She looked funny stretched out on the floor with her red book bag on her back. She reminded me of a ladybug.

I chuckled. I looked around to see if anyone else thought it was funny. I saw that Donna was red hot and mad. I tried to hide behind someone, but it was too late. Donna stood up and pushed me— for no reason.

"Hey, don't push me! It's not my fault you fell," I yelled, pushing her back.

Then know-it-all Donna ran back into the classroom screaming, "I'm gonna tell! Ms. Newel! Ms. Newel, Tiger pushed me! Tiger made me fall and tear my tights."

"Rrrr." I was not going to let her get away with this. "Ms. Newel, that's not true! I didn't push her!"

"Yes you did!" argued Miss
Smarty-Pants.

Ms. Newel ran over and stood
between Donna and me. She looked
like a baseball umpire calling a
steal "safe!" Instead, Ms. Newel was
calling, "Silence!" Ms. Newel sat us
down in chairs by her desk.

It took the know-it-all forever to tell what she thought happened. I told my side in one measly minute.

"Ms. Newel, I'd never push somebody down and not say I'm sorry," I reasoned.

"That's enough," said Ms. Newel, who's usually a jewel. "Apologize to each other and shake hands before you miss the bus."

Rrrr, as if touching Donna Overton once wasn't bad enough!

Ms. Newel walked Donna and me to the bus ramp. Donna kept whining about those silly tights being torn. Maybe if they weren't so tight, they wouldn't have torn.

I didn't like being walked to my

bus, and I didn't like being last. As
I got closer to bus number 1619, I
could feel a hundred eyeballs
gazing at me.

No Milk = No Cereal

The next morning, I had forgotten about the whole Donna thing. I had more important things to think about. A new box of cereal! I made up a rap while I was getting a bowl.

Crunch, bunch, lunch, munch,
Cereal goes crunch.
I like this stuff a bunch.
For breakfast or for lunch,
It's so goo-od to munch.

First things first! I dug my whole arm into the cereal box. The toy usually sinks to the bottom, but I couldn't find it. So I got the big bowl my mom uses for making cakes. I poured the cereal into the bowl. Well, at least most of it. Some of the cereal landed on the table. The last thing to fall out was the toy.

"Rrrr," I roared—it was only a spin top.

I heard Mom coming downstairs. I had to put the cereal back in the box. I held the bowl under the edge of the table.

With my other arm, I slid the
spilled cereal into it. It worked!
Then I lifted the big bowl over the
box and started to pour. Cereal
flew everywhere—out of the bowl,
over the table, onto the floor! Oops.

Crunch! Mom stopped before

taking another step. It was like
she'd seen a rat or something run
across the kitchen floor. She took
two more steps.

Crunch, crunch!

Mom looked down at her feet.
Then she looked up at me. I looked
down at her feet as if I had no idea
what was going on. She was looking
a lot upset.

"Tiger! What in the world?"
When Mom talks with her teeth
grinding, she means business.
"Tiger, fetch the broom!" yelled Mom
as she grabbed the bowl from me.

Instead, I opened the refrigerator
door. "Milk? Where's the milk?
Mom? Are we out of milk?"

"Yes, Tiger, we are out of milk. Now get the broom!"

"Rrrr, " I roared. I really wanted cereal. A beautiful morning had quickly turned ugly.

"Don't growl at me. You should've checked for milk first.

Just eat it dry. You've got to hurry. You have a lot of sweeping to do!" said Mom.

I didn't want to eat dry cereal. I thought about adding water. Yuck!

By the time I ate the dry cereal, drank my juice, and cleaned up the mess, it was really late. I couldn't

believe Mom expected me to sweep.
That took extra, extra long.
Sweeping is major punishment for
a seven-year-old. I grabbed my
backpack and lunch. Then I flew
out the door and ran down the
driveway.

My mom came running behind
me. "Oh, nooo!" I knew what she
was planning to do.

Why couldn't she have done her
good-bye kissing in the house?
I thought about
running faster, but I
knew she'd be sad.
So I stopped and let
her give me a quick
kiss.

I hoped my best friends, Ted and Fred, didn't see "the kiss." They're much older than me. They're in third grade and probably don't get baby kisses.

Girl Jail

After wiping off Mom's totally embarrassing kiss, I got on the bus. I walked to my favorite seat with my head hanging down. If anybody (especially Ted or Fred) was making faces at me, I didn't want to see it.

Even though we get our own seats, Ted and Fred still sit together. It must be because they're twins.

"Are you wearing lipstick,

Tiger?" snickered Ted while Fred made lip-smacking noises.

Just then, the bus turned onto a new street. I was saved from Ted and Fred's joke. I slid over in my seat to see where we were going. Our bus stopped next to another bus.

Mr. Knight stood up and said, "Boys and girls, please move over. We're going to help these kids get to school."

Oh no! Where were they gonna sit? Before I had time to blink, kids started piling onto the bus.

"Rrrr!" I roared at one kid who eyed my seat. First, no milk. Then Mom babying me. Now I had to share my seat.

I tried to take up as much room as possible. A little girl tried to squeeze in on the edge.

"Tiger, please slide over. We're going to have to sit three to a seat," said Mr. Knight.

"Thrrree," I roared. I would have rather sat on the dirty floor. In anger, I kicked my feet up against the back of the seat in front of me and slid over.

"Hey, Tiger," said Ted, looking over the back of his seat, "what's wrong? A few more girl germs aren't gonna hurt."

Just then, I spotted the know-it-all! I tried to duck, but it was too late! Donna sat down on the other side of the little girl. I could feel Donna's eyeballs looking at me. I shifted my body up against the window and began banging my forehead on the cold glass. I knew I looked like a nut. But that's exactly how I felt sitting beside two girls. I was definitely in girl jail.

Donna sucked her teeth and mumbled something.

"Did you say something?" I asked the little girl.

"I didn't say nothing," said the little girl.

"Is that Tiger boy messing with you?" Donna asked in her usual bossy voice.

"Nobody's talking to you, Donna!"

"Well, nobody's talking to you either, Tiger!"

Bus seats are not made for three people, especially not two girls and one boy. I couldn't wait to get to school so I could get out of girl jail.

Name Art

"Art class, here I come!" I sang as the bus pulled up to our school. On Wednesday and Friday mornings, I have art class. I love art class because Ms. Rice is the teacher. She is cool, pretty, and not old.

When Donna and I went into our classroom, Ms. Newel was sitting at her desk reading a book. Our class had already gone to art!

"Oh, no! I'm late!" I took off down the hall.

"Tiger Turcotte! Donna Overton! No running in the halls!" yelled Ms. Newel.

I realized that Donna Overton was right behind me.

"You won't be able to catch me," I called over my shoulder. But then

I thought about walking into the art room with bossy Donna.
It might look like we were friends or something.

I slowed down. Donna smirked as she passed me. I counted to fifty and slowly walked into the art room alone.

I love the art room. It's cheerful and colorful. There's a trillion mobiles hanging from the ceiling. Sometimes it's neat gazing at the mobiles that swish around like kites in the wind.

The other kids were busy working.

"Tiger, Donna, please sit next to each other so I can explain your project," said Ms. Rice.

"Do I have to sit beside Donna?"

"Is there a problem?" asked
Ms. Rice.

"Yeah! Is there a problem?"
echoed snotty-faced Donna Overton.

"Tiger and Donna, I'd like you to
draw your initials on a big piece of
construction paper."

"I want pink!" demanded Donna.

"I want orange. Please!" I asked
Ms. Rice in a nice way.

"Decorate the inside of the letters
using lots of colors, shapes, and
creative designs," instructed
Ms. Rice.

I got started on my letters as
soon as Ms. Rice left our table.
First, I drew a large letter *T* on my

paper with a black marker. Then I carefully drew black tiger stripes inside the *T*.

"Tiger, give me that black marker!" demanded bossy Donna. Of course, I didn't pay her any mind.

"Tiger, give me the black marker!"

I held up the marker and said, "This one? I'm using it. I'll think about giving it to you when I finish."

I went back to drawing my other *T*. Slowly I drew lots of tiny tiger paws inside. After I finished with the black marker, I rolled it down the table to Donna. It wasn't my fault that she didn't see the marker roll past her before it hit the floor.

I barely glanced up at Donna. I knew it made her mad, and so I was kinda glad.

Later, I decided to use some crayons, but Donna was hogging the colors I needed. I looked over at Phillip's table to see if they had any crayons. Nope.

"Donna, I need the black and brown," I said pointing to the huge pile of crayons in front of her. She didn't budge or answer. She completely ignored me.

"Hey girl, I need to use the black and brown crayons!" I knew she heard me, but I decided to chill.

Nothing can spoil art class—I love to draw. Sometimes drawing gets me in trouble, like when I draw in my regular class. Ms. Newel (who is sometimes not a jewel) says, "If you're drawing, you're not listening." But that's not true. I hear perfectly fine when I'm drawing.

Once Ms. Rice told me she used to get in trouble for drawing instead of doing classwork. That's another reason why I like Ms. Rice. We both love to draw.

Ms. Rice is really nice.
I think I'll say it twice.
Ms. Rice is really nice.

There's another reason why Ms. Rice is my favorite teacher. Sometimes she plays popular music in class, like songs I've heard on the radio.

The music Ms. Rice was playing made me want to wiggle in my seat. Some of my friends were nodding their heads and tapping their feet. Another neat thing about art class is

that we get to laugh out loud and whisper while we work. We can't do any of that stuff in our regular class. We'd end up in after-school detention for life.

I was minding my own business drawing two capital *T*s and listening to music. All of a sudden, Donna Overton called me, "Tiger Toilet."

I was so mad that my hand started shaking.

"You make me so-o-o-o sick!" I said quietly to myself, because I couldn't think of anything good to call her back.

At first, I thought about saying, "Donna's so fat she weighs over a ton." But then, I realized how stupid that would make me sound. The know-it-all is tall and skinny like a toothpick.

Instead, I threw my hand right up in her face. "In your face 'cause you're a disgrace!" I said right on time but way too loud.

"Donna and Tiger, you're talking too loud and too much. You are supposed to be working, not talking or name-calling," warned Ms. Rice.

The other kids snickered.

"Sorry, Ms. Rice," said sneaky Donna.

As soon as Ms. Rice walked away, Donna Overton started up again. "Your initials look stupid," she said.

At first, I ignored her little comments, but my blood was starting to boil.

"T, T, T, uh, T, T, uh, Tiger Toilet, Tiger teed on the toilet," she said.

That did it! I glanced at Donna's drawing. To my surprise, I had figured out a comeback. I smiled at her with revenge smeared all over my face.

All eyes were glued on me.

Donna looked at me like, "What's your problema?"

"Donna Overton, your initials are D.O. because your head is shaped like a DOnut. Ha, ha, ha! Ha, ha, ha!" I giggled out of control.

I had the class rolling. Everyone was laughing. The guys, especially Phillip and D'Andre, grinned with victory written across their faces. The germy girls stood up and watched with their arms folded at their waist.

Donna was so mad, she couldn't open her mouth to say anything.

In a way, it was like playing a game, boys against the germy girls. But I, Tiger  Turcotte, silenced Miss Bossy, Donut-Head Donna. Telling her off was the most fun I'd had this year. I hoped she would leave me alone forever.

5

Caught

I was so busy telling off Donna, I didn't notice that Ms. Rice was standing right behind me. There was no way I could have gotten out of the situation.

"Go out into the hall," said Ms. Rice.

Miss know-it-all DO-nut Girl started crying before Ms. Rice even slammed the door. Why waste tears over something your parents won't know about? I was ready to act like a man. Besides, Ms. Rice liked me.

"Ms. Rice, I couldn't help it. Donna started it. This was not my fault." I explained.

Donna stopped crying and stared at me. I stared back at her. If she

was spittin' mad, so was I. We looked like boxers getting ready to throw down.

Ms. Rice put her hands on her waist. "Uh, oh!" I said to myself. I hadn't seen that side of Ms. Rice before.

"Don't even think about lunch detention. You two are in deeper trouble than you think. Both of you were warned, but no-o-o, you didn't pay me any mind. The two of you continued to disturb my class."

Ms. Rice walked back and forth in front of Donna and me. She was real mad. Ms. Rice said in a very mean and loud voice, "I'm going to give you after-school detention!"

Ms. Rice handed us after-school detention slips. "Give this note to your parents."

"Do our parents have to see the note?" I interrupted.

"What do you think?" said Ms. Rice.

Oh no, she didn't! It felt like Ms. Rice dissed me. After Ms. Rice said that, you-know-who began snickering. "Why did I let smelly Donna get me in trouble?" I said under my breath.

Unfortunately, Ms. Rice thought I was talking back. She sent Donna back into the classroom.

"Why do I have to stay out here? Come on Ms. Rice, be real. What did I do this time?" I tried acting hip with her, but it didn't work. She just got madder. I held my head down and closed my mouth.

Ms. Rice made me stay out in the hall for the rest of art class. I didn't get to finish my masterpiece. I was all alone in the hall. I was mad, mad at Donna Donut-Head and Ms. Rice (my ex-favorite art teacher).

Then came the hard part—going home with my first after-school detention slip.

6

The Signature

The rest of the school day zipped by. Any other day would have moved slowly. But no-o-o, it was the quickest afternoon in my whole life. I spent the day thinking about what my parents were going to do with me when they found out.

I wondered if they'd kick me out of the house. Maybe they would ground me until summer. What if

I couldn't have bubble gum ice cream for a year? What if they took away all of my tiger stuff? What if they made me go to school on Saturdays?

If they had bought milk, my day wouldn't have been so bad!

On the way to my bus, I passed the broken-down bus from this morning. And guess whose big head was pressed up to the window? Donut-Head, and she was waving at me with a big grin on her face. Donna Overton had the nerve to wave at me!

Then she shouted, "See you tomorrow, Tiger!" like she was happy about being in after-school

detention.

What was
up with that?
Maybe she
was glad that I got in trouble. She
was weird, smelly, and wicked.

When I got home, both my
parents were home.

"Hi, Tiger! How was your day?"
said Mom.

I was so nervous. I thought
about saying it was okay.

"Well, what happened? Did
you learn anything new today?"
asked Dad.

Boy did I! I learned that girls are
like germs—they're bad news.
Don't let them touch you, breathe

on you, or get too close. Girls love to get us boys in trouble.

My mouth was really dry. I could hardly swallow. I cleared my throat and tried facing the truth.

"Donna Overton made fun of me today. She called me some very ugly names. And, well, I called her some names back. It wasn't all my fault. Donna wanted the black marker and got mad because I was using it. Then she wouldn't let me borrow the crayons. She had more crayons than anybody. Donna started the whole thing. I guess she just doesn't like me. We both got in trouble," I said really fast.

"Tiger, you know better," said Mom.

"Ms. Rice says you have to sign this," I handed Dad the slip

"Detention!" said Dad.

"Tiger, how could you do that in your favorite teacher's class?" asked Mom.

"She was my favorite teacher, but not anymore," I said in a sad, quiet voice. I was seeking as much pity as I could possibly get.

Mom and Dad looked at me with disappointment. That made me feel really bad. I don't like making my parents (especially my mom) feel bad about something I've done.

"Go to your room," said my parents at the same time.

In slow motion, I headed to my room, then asked, "But for how long? It wasn't all my fault! It was just a little bit my fault."

"Tiger, come back here," directed my dad. "Have a seat right here beside your old man."

Oops. I hoped my complaining hadn't landed me in hotter water. I may never get to play computer games for the rest of my life.

"Tiger, you are old enough to take more responsibility for your actions," explained Dad.

"I agree!" said Mom.

I looked at Mom with a sad face because she wasn't on my side.

"Tiger, I know you haven't forgotten about this morning."

"No ma'am. But I can't help that we were out of milk!"

"Tiger! The milk didn't cause the mess," corrected Mom.

"Tiger, we are not going to drag this thing out, but you need to accept responsibility when you are at fault. Nobody is perfect. We've all made mistakes," said Dad.

"That's right! Your dad has had to apologize many times for saying the wrong thing during a disagreement," said Mom while winking at my dad.

"Learn from your mistakes, son. Try working on your attitude toward girls, especially Donna. Remember, your mom used to be a germy girl. Now look at her. She has lost just about all of her yucky germs," laughed Dad.

They still made me go to my room for a hundred years. Or at least, it felt like a hundred years. It hurt, but it also felt good being honest.

For punishment, my parents didn't kick me out in the cold after all. I had to stay indoors the entire weekend. I couldn't go outside and ride my scooter. I couldn't have any company. I couldn't watch TV,

and I couldn't play with any
computer or electronic games. Not
bad but boring, boring, boring.

After-School Detention

7

The next day came too fast. I was feeling nervous about after-school detention. I wondered if I should fake a stomachache. But I knew my mom would not believe me.

In the lunch line, Donna dropped her straw and I gave her a new one.

"Thanks!" Donna said politely with a small smile. I felt stupid after being nice. I hoped none of the guys saw me being nice to a girl.

After lunch, Ms. Newel gave me a sticker shaped like a big star.

"Tiger, that was a very kind thing you did in the lunch line for Donna. I heard you two had a little trouble yesterday. Here's a 'Caught You Being Good' sticker."

Ms. Newel made me feel good about being nice. Maybe yesterday was just a bad day. Whether it was or not, I didn't plan on getting in any more trouble.

When Yaka asked, "Do you have an eraser?" I let her borrow mine.

D'Andre looked at me with a

surprised smirk. "What's up with that, Tiger?"

I smiled and shook my head.

At the end of the day, I nervously waited for the bell to ring. "Ring, Ring-a-ling, Ring." The bell rang, and all the kids rushed out the door.

Next, Ms. Rice came into the classroom. "Hello, Tiger and Donna. Gather your things and come with me." We picked up our backpacks and followed Ms. Rice to the art room.

"Tiger and Donna, I'm going to allow you to finish your name art

assignment." Maybe Ms. Rice
would still be my favorite teacher.

Part of my punishment included
an apology. Yeah, that's right. My
mom and dad told me to apologize
to Ms. Rice and Donna Overton.
"We're expecting you to handle
yourself like a Turcotte."

I didn't mind apologizing to Ms.
Rice. I did disturb her class. But
apologizing to Donna . . . I honestly
didn't want to do. I just didn't
think it was fair unless she
apologized to me first.

"Ms. Rice, I'm sorry for cutting
up in your class yesterday. I'll try
very hard not to disturb your class
anymore."

"I appreciate and accept your apology," said Ms. Rice with a sparkle in her smile.

After I apologized to Ms. Rice, I walked over to Donna's table. She acted like I was invisible. I whispered, "I'm sorry for calling you a name." Then I ran back to my table.

"Whew, that was germinator tough," I said wiping my forehead.

Did Donna Overton apologize to me? No, and I wouldn't be holding my breath waiting for her to either. I guessed her parents don't care about her character the way my folks do.

Donna and I helped Ms. Rice hang the name art posters from our class in the hall. Donna and I actually worked together with no problems.

"Tiger, could you tear me off a piece of tape?"

"Sure," I answered Donna.

We hung them on the wall beside Ms. Rice's door. It felt kinda strange—me, Donna, and Ms. Rice being back out in the hall together.

When we finished, Ms. Rice said, "Look at all these beautiful name art posters. It shows you all are proud of your names, and you should be."

"Tiger, your teasing me yesterday

ended up giving me an idea."

I glared at Donna's poster.

"It's the O silly. It's a strawberry frosted donut with sprinkles. Get it?" said Donna.

"Oh, yeah! That's a nice donut. You're a good donut drawer."

I wondered why I didn't see that yesterday. I guess I was too busy being the Germinator.

The Girl Jail Remix

We went back into the art room. Ms. Rice explained, "Tiger and Donna, part of after-school detention involves thinking about why you ended up in after-school detention."

The fun was over, I thought. Fifteen minutes would feel like fifteen hours. I knew everybody hated after-school detention for a reason.

"Donna, we have something in common," said Ms. Rice.

"We do?" Donna asked with surprise.

"Yes! Our first name starts with the same letter."

Then Ms. Rice told us about how kids used to tease her in third grade. Her first name is Darby. It's pronounced like Barbie except with a *D*.

"Most of the kids in Virginia had southern accents. When they pronounced my name, it sounded like 'dirty rice.' I believed the kids called me that on purpose.

It used to make me so upset," explained Ms. Rice. "But my grandma set me straight. She said, 'Darby darling, your name was one of the first gifts you received from your parents. Always honor and cherish your name.'"

"I think I know how you felt," I agreed. "In kindergarten, everybody thought my name was a joke. My two best friends bet that Tiger wasn't my real name."

"I've never had anybody joke about my name. Well, that was until yesterday," joined Donna.

I started to feel sad. Then I couldn't believe my ears.

"I'm sorry for treating you like a meanie, Tiger. I just wanted to see if you would get mad. You know real tigers have a temper," joked Donna.

"Well now, I think after-school detention has been successfully served. It's time to call it a day!" said Ms. Rice, gathering her bags.

Ms. Rice's story got me thinking about how I got my name. I was named after my grandpa. My parents said that the Turcotte name was a respected name. I had to keep respect in our family. "Pass it on to your kids one day, Tiger." said my dad.

Ms. Rice led us outside to wait for

our parents. Donna had the nerve to sit beside me on the curb. I just knew she had something up her sleeve.

I tried ignoring her and went on digging in a hole with a twig. Then, for the first time, I actually looked at her face. Donna smiled at me. What for, I had no idea.

I slid over to the right creating a bigger space between Donna and me. Phillip and D'Andre would go wild if they saw me sitting on a curb close to a girl. But then, Donna copied me and moved closer to the right.

"Tiger, I think your name is neat," said Donna.

I was going to die. I felt shaky

and weak. I was definitely in girl jail again. But it actually wasn't so bad. And I thought of a new rap.

I've got to stay cool,
Like a slow moving cow.
Can't open my mouth,
Can't say a word now.

I noticed my mom's car pulling up to the school. Our car was blue, but for some reason, it looked green. My head was spinning, and I felt like I couldn't breathe. I was ready to go. I stood up, grabbed my backpack, and wished my mom would hurry up.

"Tiger seems to be in a hurry," Mom said to Ms. Rice with a smile.

"It has been a long day," agreed Ms. Rice.

I left without saying good-bye. I jumped in our car and shut the door.

"Is something wrong?" asked Mom with concern.

I smiled and said, "No." Secretly, I had a big grin on the inside.

I thought about my name on the way home. Grandpa was born with  very large hands and feet. He reminded his parents of a baby tiger. My great-grandpa had a deep love for tigers. So that's where the name Tiger came from.

It's a good thing Grandpa didn't
have an extra big head or butt.
Great-grandpa and Grandma
might have named him Hippo
Turcotte. Mom looked at me with a
strange smirk.

"What's so funny?" she asked.

"Oh, nothing," I said, but that wasn't all true. By the time we pulled into the driveway, I had a new rap in my head.

Thinking about my friend,
I'd never tell Ted or Fred.
Their teasing would never end.
I'll be the only one to know,
I kinda like that girl D.O.
So now I gotta go.
Peace!
Rrr.